Max's Job

by Katherine Scraper • illustrated by Richard Harrington

Meet the Characters

Max

Mom

Dad

sister

Max loved to shovel snow.
Max could shovel snow faster
than anyone. He shoveled
the snow for all his neighbors.

Now Max was waiting for the snow. Max looked out the window every day. The snow did not come.

Max looked at the sky every day.
The snow did not come.

7

Max asked, "Mom, when will we have snow? I cannot do my job!"

Mom said, "You could be a dog walker."

Max did not want to be
a dog walker. He asked his
dad, "When will we have snow?
I cannot do my job!"
Dad said, "You could
be a paperboy."

Max did not want to be
a paperboy.

"When will we have snow? I
need to do my job!" he said to
his sister.

"You could be a babysitter,"
said his sister.

Max was sad.

He took off his coat.

He took off his hat, too.

"I need a new job," he said.

Then Max looked out the window.

"SNOW!!!" he yelled.

"I love my job!" said Max.